DAN B. FIERCE

ROADKILL KING

FIERCE Imagination

Copyright ©2021 by Fierce Imagination
All rights reserved. No part of this work may be reproduced or transmitted in any form, or by any means, electronic or mechanical, including photocopying, or by any information storage and retrieval system, without permission from the author or Fierce Imagination in writing. Reviewers may quote brief passages.

This is a work of fiction. Any similarities between any persons, living or deceased, or any place is purely coincidental. No animals were harmed.

Cover Design by Angel Esqueda and Angel Creative Web Design

CONTENTS

Acknowledgments	vii
Chapter 1	1
Chapter 2	5
Chapter 3	9
Chapter 4	13
Chapter 5	17
Chapter 6	23
Chapter 7	29
Contact Me	33
Links	35
Also by Dan B. Fierce	37
Also by Dan B. Fierce	39
About the Author	41

DEDICATION

This short story is dedicated to my husband, Brian, my family, friends, fellow authors in my circle, and coworkers.
You all put up with my twisted imagination, flakiness, and procrastination. (More about that later.)
This small victory is as much yours as it is mine.
Thank you all for being my support base.
I love you all.

ACKNOWLEDGMENTS

Special thanks to Mustang Patty, Moaner Lawrence, Christienne Gillespie, Angel Esqueda, Angelique Anderson, Dean Boese, and Sarah Stewart for your help in perfecting this story.

CHAPTER ONE

Tatum Johnson wiped his pride and joy down with a chamois. This car, his baby, only saw any action when he got "the itch," a need deep inside of him to go hunting. That was what he called it: hunting. The truth was no amount of scrubbing or buffing could rid his monstrous creation of the stains that peppered its grill. Or its driver's soul.

He knew what he was doing when building this machine. Initially, Tatum didn't spend too much on the Ford Mustang GT, knowing that he would have to gut and rebuild the whole thing. He found an ad on Craigslist: some poor kid who needed to get rid of the car fast and cheap.

Every spare penny he had went into rebuilding the Coyote 5.0 engine, reinforcing the side panels, and placing a protective cage around the grill and intake. The bulletproof, shatterproof windshield nearly broke the bank, not to mention sent up a ton of unwanted red flags to certain law agencies. If they ever visited, he'd just tell them it was only for shows. With a bulldozer-like spiked scoop in front and steel plates riveted in place, it looked more akin to a car from a dystopian movie. The disabled airbags and safety features disqualified it from being street legal. A steel skid plate protected the bottom of the chassis from getting damaged when he found his prey.

The car started as a matte black, but Tatum's hobby had given it a crimson splatter pattern that he grew to love through the years. So rather than wash off the evidence, he would rub it in, sniffing the viscera as a chef would his special dish. Then, he'd allow it to dry, only removing the grit that gave any poor animal ample warning of encroaching death.

Spring and fall were his favorite seasons, but especially spring. As animals came out of hibernation, most of them rarely recalled the need for caution as they crossed roads at night. The critters' minds were on baser needs, like food or finding a mate. Most people seemed to go out of their way, even wreck their cars, to prevent killing innocent creatures. Not Tatum. It was his hobby, his form of hunting. He would practically destroy his vehicle to hit the innocent beings.

"Come on, baby. Let's see if Daddy can find you something to eat." He missed the roar it used to have when cranking the car into life. Tatum figured out quieting the exhaust made his expeditions more successful.

He pulled the car into the street to go through Attenborough as the sun set. "This town's name is longer than its main street," he muttered to himself, "but not nearly as long as the local gossip chain's attention span." People craned their necks as he sped by. He could see them in his rearview mirror, wagging their tongues about what he did with the car, some of them so far off-base with their stories, it was amusing when it finally got back to him. It even earned him a nickname: the Roadkill King. He relished their stares, a sadistic sneer on his face as he spied them in his peripheral. "They think I snapped after Jessica dumped me. What the hell do they know?"

At the edge of town, he saw her. Jessica Jessup. Part of him still loved her—the "other" part of him. She was crossing the street from the vet's office where she worked, watching over the sick or boarded pets overnight. Her dinner order was likely waiting for her in the café on the corner. Then an uncontrollable urge overcame him.

He stomped on the gas, tires squealing, and smoke rising from the pavement. The final block between them closed in a flash. There wasn't even time for a shriek. Tatum was sure he saw her emerald-green eyes pass the windshield in a frozen stare of disbelief as his car scooped her from the road with a series of thumps. Skidding the vehicle around to face the direction he came from, his heart raced with glorious victory, his prize catch laying lifeless in the street.

"No one kicks me to the curb," he chuckled as Jessica's body lay in a rapidly growing crimson pool. Onlookers screamed out their shock. Motorists wailed on their horns in protest.

The truck behind him honked impatiently, waking Tatum from his perverse daydream. "You waiting for the stop sign to turn green, Tate?"

He saw Jessica look down the street towards the commotion, shocked, and heart likely racing at the excitement. Then, finally, she hurried to the sidewalk, a frightened, uncertain look on her face. Tatum felt an odd mixture of relief and disappointment as Jessica vanished into the restaurant.

He glowered at his mirror to see who was causing the unwanted attention. "James Bridger. I hope you bring your little dick-mobile to my shop again soon."

CHAPTER TWO

His mind flew into another daydream. Tatum was working on James's vehicle. Cutting the brake lines as it sat prone on the lift, he frayed them to make them appear less surgical and more incidental. After his diesel truck roared to life and money exchanged hands, Bridger would thank him and likely drive off with a hillbilly holler. Eventually, the unfortunate man would be found dead, his four-wheel-drive Chevy going over a guard rail before toppling over the side of a cliff in a spectacular action movie sequence of wreckage and explosion.

"Come on, Mad Max!" James shouted with another blare of his horn. "Move that contraption!"

Tatum shook off the notion and stuck out his left hand, proffering a "New York hello" with his middle finger to the asshole in the jacked-up truck.

Taking a deep breath, Tatum finished his trek across the street moving onto the crunching gravel of the country roads, his hunting grounds. The sun was starting to hide behind the horizon. Primetime hunting would soon begin. Besides, he had to make himself scarce or risk gaining the attention of "Sheriff Dingus." The last time he and the lawman crossed paths, it took a silver tongue and an act of God to keep from getting a ticket over his ride. Of course, being the only auto shop in a small town also helped, especially when the local police force wanted all of their oil changes at no charge.

Hours passed as the light waned into a starry evening. "I hate slow nights." Tatum groaned, gripping the steering wheel with white-knuckled agitation. He had gone for days without so much as a rustle of the ditch weed by the road. After an extended dry spell like this, he would get edgier until his attitude leaked over into his day-to-day life. "At this point, I'd even settle for a skunk. It took me the better part of a day to get that smell off last time. Damned near lost my paint job."

The sight of Jessica popped back into his head as his tires crunched on the lonely gravel road. A sneer crossed his lips while his mind flashed back to that fateful night. He knew she had a soft heart for animals, a kindness he would never share. She was a vet tech, after all. Having just hit a golden retriever in front of its house, he pulled over to the side of the road.

"Let's go, baby, before the owner comes out." His pulse raced and fists clenched as he bounced from one foot to the other.

Jessica shot him a baleful glare as if he had done it on purpose. "If I can save this dog's life, I will! Go see if the owners are home." The dog whistled a barely audible whine as she cradled its bleeding skull.

Tatum loved Jessica, but he never cared much for animals of any kind. The way she looked at him made him hate that stupid canine for darting into the street. He didn't mean to hit the dog; it just happened. The critter was probably after something or wanted to chase his car.

"It's not my fault," he muttered. He only got two steps onto the driveway when he saw the boy standing there in a stupor, his mouth a frozen "O" of terror. Tate looked at the kid, momentarily speechless. "Oh, shit. Look, kid..."

The child's brain and body released as he screeched and ran to his dog, dropping the ball in his hand to the ground absently. "Bucky! What did you do to Bucky, you asshole?"

Tatum wasn't sure how the kid ran with a river of tears streaming from his eyes, but the boy's cursing only served to flare his anger. He felt horrible about the accident. The parents soon joined their wailing offspring, the father quickly clutching his wife's face to his chest as she lamented. Jessica did what she could; the dog's injuries were too severe.

The day she delivered their beloved pet's ashes back to the family, she made Tatum go with her. It was all he heard about for a week straight. By then, his anguish over the mishap morphed into an absolute, black hatred for the family and their stupid dog. Nevertheless, he went along, thinking it would at least keep him in Jessica's good graces. Afterward, his final apology to his beloved felt more robotic than sincere.

She broke up with him the next day.

CHAPTER THREE

A pair of eyes shone at the side of the road almost a mile away. The mechanic's breath hitched, bringing him back to the present. Tatum could barely make out a silhouette at this distance. Whatever it was stood far taller than the raccoons, opossums, dogs, and cats he usually saw. The glowing eyes dipped toward the ground for a few seconds and then arched back up, gleaming in his direction. He slowed the car to a stop at about half the distance. Then, flipping a switch, his headlights went from a bright halogen to a soft, greenish hue.

"A deer!" He took a closer look as antlers flashed in his headlights. "A buck. A big one, too!"

His heart raced with anticipation. Tatum salivated at the chance he was being given. Slowly, he pulled on his night-vision goggles as if the slightest movement might spook away his opportunity.

"Now, let's see what this baby can do." He had hoped for some "big game" this year. The last time he hit a deer, it took thousands of dollars and several weeks of repairs. Reinforcing the hood and side panels, putting cages around the grill, head-lights, and windows, as well as removing the spoiler, had just been the start. The engine purred below the hood like a tiger on the prowl. "Come on, big guy," he coaxed, willing the animal to wander into the road as a hunter would train his sites on his target. "You can do it. Just a few more steps."

The majestic creature did precisely as Tatum had expected. The buck's pace was slow and cautious as he strolled over the steep ditch onto the gravel pathway. The mechanic would have to close the distance fast without spooking the animal. His foot shoved the pedal to the floorboard, spraying an assault of rock behind him. Tate corrected the car as it fish-tailed, holding it straight after a few seconds. Rocks fanned out behind the Mustang as his speedometer climbed. He held one finger on the light switch to flip them back to halogen and freeze his prey in place. He didn't have time to react. The road where the buck stood was uneven. It dipped and ebbed like an ocean wave, causing him to lose control of the vehicle.

The car swerved and spun, striking the buck with its side. Glass from the driver's side window shattered, spraying Tatum in the face. The muscle car swerved in a complete circle before tumbling like a gymnast, coming to rest in a field, landing on its passenger's side. The wheels spun as the car rocked into its final resting place. It took several minutes of hanging on his side by the seat belt before Tatum caught his bearings. Shaking the glass off, blood sprayed from a gash on his forehead as his mind wobbled, unable to focus.

Then, finally, he groggily turned his head and got the shock of his life as he nearly skewered his face on the buck's mangled, protruding rack. It had wedged itself in the cage surrounding the window during the impact. Now all 250 pounds of the creature hung limp like a dish towel and in an awful, twisted heap over his still teetering car.

"Fuck." Tatum tried the door almost instinctively, but the animal's added weight prevented escape in that direction. He pondered the still flawless windshield. "Kinda screwed myself with the shatterproof glass. Can't get out there." He studied his surroundings. All he saw was a groove of upheaved dirt from his car on the passenger side. "First things first." He tried to unbuckle the belt, but his weight kept it locked tight. Reaching into his pocket, the mechanic drew out a small knife and sawed at the sturdy fabric weakly.

Just as Tatum was about to make the final stroke, the buck snorted to life, causing him to scream. The creature's eyes showed no signs of life. Instead, the irises had gone entirely crimson.

CHAPTER FOUR

"Holy Fuck!"

The seatbelt gave with an audible snap, sending the wide-eyed mechanic crumbling in a heap onto his head and shoulders into gravity's embrace. The stag kicked and snorted, rocking the car violently, wobbling it back and forth. Tatum sucked in air from the impact and cradled the back of his head. The mechanic tossed about like a sock in the dryer while the suffering animal frantically snorted and yanked.

"Juh..." The buck ggrruuffed as it rocked the car, still trying to free itself from the window's cage. "Johnson."

Did he just speak? Did that deer just say my last name?

The pendulating of the car increased. Backward. Pause for inertia. Forward. Another pause.

The hesitations lengthened, threatening to either right the vehicle or set it on its roof. Metal creaked and groaned as Tatum's prized possession swung.

"Tay." The buck huffed in one final grunt of massive effort. "Tum."

The car swung down. The stag landed on all fours. Then, ripping the door from its hinges with a mighty tug of its horns, the creature sent it sailing into the woods like a frisbee, where it wrapped itself around an oak before clattering to the ground. The Mustang crashed onto its radials, bursting all four tires at once like party balloons.

The rough ride wasn't much kinder to its driver, launching him from the muscle car like a cannonball. He planted on his face, skidding like a base runner stealing home, without any of the skill or grace. Flashes of white accompanied a snap as Tatum's nose plowed into a buried rock. Lifting his head, he spat out the bloodied clump of grass he'd unearthed. His trembling hand reached for his nose, expecting it to be gushing blood, perhaps even be gone. Instead, it was there, askew from the impact, but he wasn't leaking his essence.

Must've clogged it up with dirt.

"Tatum Johnson."

The mechanic flopped over, wide-eyed, and pedaled backward, away from the booming voice. Specks of dirt washed from his eyes in muddy tears. All he could make out was a brown and white blotch looming over him. His eyesight blurry, the deer nudged him impatiently with his antlers.

"Get up. Your fate awaits."

Tatum climbed achingly to his feet, the world spinning around him. "My... Fate?"

"Unless you know another reason you'd be talking to a deer you just hit with your car."

The final bits of grit left, clearing his vision. Thunder boomed in the distance. He shook his head as he stared at the animal. Bits of bone protruded from several parts of its legs and abdomen. With each step, intestines roped out until they dragged on the ground. Its jaw was deformed and dangling askew. Still, the voice echoed in his head when it spoke without moving its mouth.

"Walk down this road until you reach a bridge."

He hesitated. Another clap of thunder shook the trees. "It's about to rain. Why don't I just take shelter in that-"

Was that cabin there before?

"Walk." The authority in the stag's voice rattled the mechanic to his core. The buck stabbed him in the backside with the broken point of an antler, causing Tatum to yelp more out of surprise than injury.

Lightning flashed. The storm grew closer. Tatum shuffled down the gravel path, his hands stuffed into his pockets and shoulders slumped like a shunned child as droplets fell from the sky.

He leered up at the clouding sky and its disappearing stars. "Awesome," he muttered, returning his gaze to his feet and kicking a stone ahead of him.

A curtain of water fell on him as he left the stag behind, stopping him in his tracks. The rain was cold, chilling him to the core. His clothes became soaked within minutes; his shoes sloshed with each step. In front of him, the full moon shone through a break in the clouds as if taunting him.

"I'm going back to that cabin. Fuck this."

CHAPTER FIVE

He spun around for the shelter. The road behind him and the road in front were the same; the same trees, the same dips, and holes in the gravel, the same moon peeking through the rain-soaked clouds. He rubbed his eyes with his knuckles, his mouth agape in disbelief. Then he turned again to make sure he hadn't been hallucinating.

"How?"

He stood with his shoulders parallel to the path, checking each direction, a feeling of dread building within him. No matter which way he looked, the route remained the same. His knees nearly gave way, face paled, and stomach knotted as a sense of hopelessness washed over him. He continued comparing all directions, dumbstruck, as a trembling hand went to his bleeding mouth.

"No. No. You can't have me. No, no no nonononono!" He sprinted down the road for a hundred feet, only gaining slightly on the hilltop in front of him. The gravel stretched away from him, teasing him with an eternity doomed to kick rocks. Full-blown panic set in. His heart thudded in his chest, his mind racing faster than his car ever went.

My car! I need to find my car. I'll drive that bastard on four flats if I have to.

No matter which way he raced, the road remained a constant. His Mustang was nowhere to be found. Finally, he glanced over to the side of the path and thought he might have spied a light in a house.

"The cabin!"

He took a single step toward the light, and the ground spun so that the gravel pointed in the same direction. Tatum Johnson collapsed to his knees in the middle of the road and cried for the first time since he and Jessica called it quits. His tears joined the raindrops, the earth drinking his regret.

"You must finish your journey."

The sudden reappearance of the broken and mangled stag caused Tatum to start backward and sit in a puddle. Now, it wasn't just his tears soaking the ground as his bladder released.

"What do you want from me?"

"Finish your walk. Go to the bridge." The buck nodded in the moon's direction. "All will be revealed there."

"Am I being punished?" Tatum felt like a scolded child, his nose running in dark, muddy rivulets. His face caked with mud with each swipe. "Is this hell?"

"That is not for me to decide. But, first, you must reach the end of the road." The buck snorted, its breath clouding the chilly air. Then, just like its steamy output, the ghost vanished once more.

The mechanic sat with his arms draped around his knees and let out another flurry of sobs.

How did it come to this?

Then he remembered. It was the last time he, and the woman he had wanted to marry, had spoken.

"You work with animals. I get it. You love the beasts just like I love cars." Tatum paced in his apartment above the garage he owned. There was barely enough room for him to take two steps, but it suited his needs until recently. "But you act like I hit that dog deliberately."

"I know you didn't kill the dog on purpose." Jessica continued gathering the few belongings she'd staged at her boyfriend's place for when she stayed over. "It was the way you acted when that boy and his family were crying over their loss."

"It. Was. Just. A. Dog."

"Precisely! To you, it was just a mangy mutt." She tossed her hairdryer into the box with a hearty thud. "To them, it was a member of their family. All you cared about was the damage done to your car, your precious fucking car." She angrily shoved more toiletries into the box. "That boy will be scarred for life! He watched you hit his beloved pet." Finally, she tossed in a bottle of conditioner. It struck the dryer, the lid cracking open and spilling some of the contents. "Great."

"I didn't make them pay for the damages. So, what more do you want from me?"

"Pay for the- "She glowered at him, stunned, cutting into his soul with her eyes. "First, you're going to take that animal's remains to them with me and apologize."

Tatum grimaced at the ridiculousness of the request. "Fine," he muttered through gritted teeth, turning away from her.

"Then, you're going to get a dog. Or a cat. Or something, anything, and take care of it."

"What the fuck for?" He stomped over to the bathroom doorway.

"To show me," she said in a calm yet firm voice, "that you care for something that isn't made of metal."

"No!" He shook his head with a determined sneer. "I've never had a pet in my life, and--"

"It shows," she interrupted, placing her toothbrush atop the brimming box and shoving her way past him toward the door. "You either need to care for something besides yourself," she popped the front portal ajar, "or you don't care for me."

"Oh, this is ridiculous! Jessica!" He followed her as she spun to go down the long stairway leading up the side of the building. "Come on, baby. Let's talk this through."

She never looked back as he rushed down to stop her. As she peeled away, he tossed a pebble at her car, dinging the trunk hood. His mind, still reeling from the event, could only concentrate on how to get the damage out as her little Chevy Cavalier puttered its ancient, oily exhaust down the street. It wasn't until she was out of sight that he noticed the smattering of an audience spread throughout the small town's main square that had stopped to witness the spectacle.

After that rumor-inducing embarrassment, he became bitter. He heard the whispers around him when he took a break for lunch or while shopping at the store, even when he went into the much larger neighboring town to get parts from the auto store. It enraged him. Instead of doing as she'd asked, he wanted to hurt every living thing he saw. Hate blossomed in his heart. He wanted the animals to feel the same pain he did. He wasn't sure how, but he would make them suffer. It wasn't until he saw that squirrel playing in the road that he came up with the perfect plan.

He had slowed down at first to let the little tree rat cross. Then he punched the pedal to the floor, mowing it down under his tire with a satisfying crunch. His need to experience that feeling again grew.

CHAPTER SIX

In the beginning, his Mustang ran fine, and the damages were minimal on the rare occasion he caught something crossing the road. After that, it became a challenge, a game, a thrill. Many a potential prey got away, but the ones that hadn't became tick marks in a small spiral notebook he kept in his glove compartment. Each type of critter had its own page.

"Four dogs," Tatum groused, licking his finger to turn the page. "Seventeen squirrels. Eight cats. I should give black cats their own page." He could recollect all of his kills, each diminutive dash on his diary of death, running down the gruesome inventory as stoically as if he were counting oil cans.

Some days, when he felt like a special outing, he'd go around, looking for specific animals. Most of the time, he just took whatever came his way, even other people's pets.

The larger animals began to cause far too many repairs, so he researched how to fortify his vehicle to fit his perverse hobby. When he hit his first fawn, it rolled up his hood and smashed the windshield. That was where the idea for the shatterproof glass came in. Sure, it was a few thousand dollars, but replacing a windscreen with modern cars would be much more costly if it happened often enough. It seemed like sound logic at the time.

The more rural the road, the more likely he'd find something to run over. He preferred pavement over gravel, but something drove him to this road on this night. Now that he wandered down it, it clicked at how unfamiliar it seemed. Then again, there were no landmarks to go by, no driveways, no mailboxes. Even the tree line didn't ring any bells.

Finally, he rounded the top of the hillside and saw the bridge. It appeared out of place in the forgotten backwoods in the dead of night. Yet, it seemed to glow, sparkling as if lit from within, spanning a ravine he not only didn't recognize but wasn't in the realm of possibility. He'd never come across it before on any of his nighttime joyrides. With each step as he approached, animals appeared from the woods, gathering at the mouth of the crossing.

There was something out of sorts about the congregation of critters. Instead of scampering and hopping to their post, they limped and dragged themselves on broken limbs, guts, bones, and organs protruding from their bodies. A squirrel that had been smashed entirely flat squirmed like an inchworm to the landing of the bridge.

There were hundreds of them. Like the flattened tree rat, all of them looked vaguely familiar. The last three to join the menagerie were unmistakable. It was the massive, muscular buck Tatum side-swiped tonight, the fawn he'd hit just last year, and finally, the one who started it all: Bucky, the golden retriever. The mechanic stood a good twenty yards from the zoo blocking the path, afraid they might attack, his eyes wide and mouth agape in horror. The buck stood sentry at the front and spoke.

"Approach, Tatum Matthew Johnson."

For several seconds, Tatum was speechless and frozen in place.

"Approach!" ordered the buck.

As the mechanic inched closer, he recognized every animal before him. Then, tears of regret began to fall anew on his face. His mind was a whirlwind, not resting on the scene long enough for it to completely hit home. "What's going on?"

"This is your Judgement, Tatum. In front of you is every animal you interacted with within your life. Before you may cross this bridge, we must evaluate your existence." Tatum's knees buckled as his heart sank, and he fell to all fours. The tears began to flow faster. Finally, the stag's voice boomed again. "Is there anyone who wishes to defend this man?"

"I will." Bucky stepped forward, a chorus of muttering behind him.

"The dog defending the human," scoffed the squirrel pancake, "Who saw that coming?"

The retriever ignored the jab and sat next to the deer, making eye contact with Tatum. The condemned man felt a spiritual connection with the dog somehow. A few seconds later, it dissipated. "I'm ready." The dog stood on all fours at attention, panting calmly, his gaze still unwavering on the man.

"Prosecution?"

The fawn ambled into view, locking eyes with Tatum, just as the canine had. Again, the mechanic felt his spirit and the animal's become one before it vanished. "I'm ready as well."

"So be it. Let's begin."

The trial was long, each animal having its say about its encounter with Tatum. The retriever plead to his client's defense, stating that this whole series of horrific events happened due to an accident and its aftermath. It was a sincere effort that fell upon deaf ears.

The buck pondered the evidence for what seemed like an eternity. "Tatum Matthew Johnson, do you have anything to add before we pass sentence?"

"I..." Tatum sputtered through heaving breaths, "I beg for forgiveness and mercy." It was all he could muster before finally breaking down. The multitude of animals chittered, squeaked, and growled in defiance.

CHAPTER SEVEN

The stag clopped his hoof like a gavel, bringing the menagerie back to silence. "You ask for forgiveness when you go out of your way to harm other living creatures? You beg for mercy after creating a vehicle designed specifically to kill?" It spun to the crowd of animals. "What say you all, my brethren?"

The flattened squirrel began to chant "guilty," the others slowly joining. Their bodies pulsated and throbbed, unifying with their verbal condemnation. Then, one by one, their corpses joined each other, merging into a tangled, fleshy mass, the "guilty" chant becoming more unified. Horror overtook Tatum. The buck was the last to bind with the demonic entity. Only the retriever refused to become one with the others.

"Run!" barked Bucky. Tatum's dumbstruck

terror engulfed his being. "I said run! Run for your soul!"

The urgency in the dog's voice freed the mechanic into flight mode as the creatures coalesced into their final form, a gigantic, muscular, veiny pink mass. Its triangular head grew a crown of antlers and broken, useless legs, and ended in a predator's beak. The skull housed four baleful, black, misaligned eyes. Two impossibly long, human-like arms, ending in powerful talons, stretched out, threatening to ensnare him.

Tatum released a shrill yowl, turning so rapidly that he lost his traction, a cartoonish and clumsy look, as his feet sputtered underneath him for purchase.

A fleshy tail jutted behind the creature like the train of a bride's gown. With each lumbering, misshapen step, pieces ripped free as it dragged itself along. A vertical slit for a mouth yawned wide. The creature bellowed a blood-curdling noise, an unearthly combination of moans and screeches in a hellish choir of voices and octaves. Row upon row of needle-like teeth gleamed in the sparse moonlight, leading into a black pit.

Panic overtook Tatum as he high-tailed it back the way he came. The road in front stretched into eternity. With each foot forward, the path teased backward double, seemingly mocking him. He was able to keep ahead of his immense pursuer, but only barely. For every three of his strides, the demon clawed at the ground only once. His heartbeat at his rib cage as if trying to escape.

As the gravel took a hairpin turn, he saw headlights. He slowed to a stop, waving frantically at the car in the distance. Relief washed over him as he began to walk toward the lights.

Clop!

The sudden change in the way his footsteps sounded sent chills up Tatum's spine. The car revved in response.

Clop. Clop.

Tatum peered downward; his legs had become those of a deer. Searing pain spiked atop his head. He groped for his noggin and felt fur and a rapidly blossoming set of horns. He clutched at them, unable to grasp what was happening. The car's lights shone on his hands as he held them in front of his face. His digits had gone missing, replaced by a set of hooves. Another jolt of agony sent him to all fours, a position that he no longer had the energy to fight. Agony wracked him as his neck stretched, and his face elongated.

Clop-clop. Clop-clop.

The vehicle in front of him revved menacingly once again. Tires screeched. Gravel sprayed behind the glowing orbs as they lurched forward, closing the distance. Before he could react, Tatum caught a brief glimpse as he pitched into the air.

The car was his, and he was behind the wheel. The world spun. Pain exploded all over his body. Glass shattered as his newly formed antlers stuck in the car's driver-side cage. He looked on in horror as his horn struck the driver deep into his neck, severing the carotid artery.

The universe went black for the briefest time.

Tatum awoke, gravity pulling him from his side, dangling him by the seat belt once again. His eyes met the buck's. There was knowledge in those eyes. That wisdom was now his to relive and forget, forever in a loop, for all of eternity.

CONTACT ME

Thank you so much for reading Roadkill King. I sincerely hope you enjoyed it. If you did, please leave a review on my Facebook Author page at: www.facebook.com/DanBFierce

I welcome feedback, comments, and critiques as well. Feel free to send them to: danfierce@yahoo.com

LINKS

Subscribe to my email newsletter for sneak peeks, updates, special offers, and even freebies! Smash the button at the bottom of the main page at:
www.firecefantoms.com

Follow me on social media as well.
Facebook: www.facebook.com/DanBFierce
Instagram: www.instagram.com/danbfierce
Twitter: @DanBFierce1

ALSO BY DAN B. FIERCE

Coming soon. Subscribe to my newsletter to get it for free.

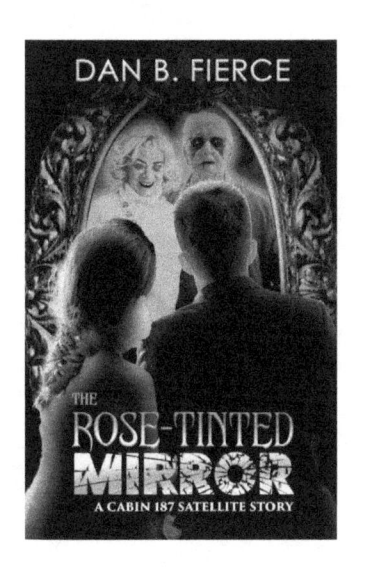

ALSO BY DAN B. FIERCE

Be sure to keep your eyes peeled for the upcoming release of the "parent" collection of short stories that inspired Roadkill King:

Cabin 187 in late 2021 or early 2022!

ABOUT THE AUTHOR

Dan B. Fierce lives in his hometown of Kansas City, Missouri, with his husband of eighteen plus years and family. He loves horror, comedy, and most things in between.

He contributed three short stories to the "2020 Indie Author's Short Story Anthology," as well as one story to "Clues and Culprits: An anthology by the Indie Author's Group," coming out on October 31st, 2021. Both can be found on Amazon.

This is his first solo publication.